DINA the RAPPER

Level 3H

Written by Lucy George
Illustrated by Andrew Geeson
Reading Consultant: Betty Franchi

About Phonics

Spoken English uses more than 40 speech sounds. Each sound is called a *phoneme*. Some phonemes relate to a single letter (d-o-g) and others to combinations of letters (sh-ar-p). When a phoneme is written down, it is called a *grapheme*. Teaching these sounds, matching them to their written form, and sounding out words for reading is the basis of phonics.

Early phonics instruction gives children the tools to sound out, blend, and say the words without having to rely on memory or guesswork. This instruction gives children the confidence and ability to read unfamiliar words, helping them progress toward independent reading.

About the Consultant

Betty Franchi is an American educator with a Bachelor's Degree in Elementary and Middle Education as well as a Master's Degree in Special Education. Betty holds a National Boards for Professional Teaching Standards certification. Throughout her 24 years as a teacher, she has studied and developed an expertise in Phonetic Awareness and has implemented phonetic strategies, teaching many young children to read, including students with special needs.

Reading tips

 This book focuses on the *er* sound as in rapper.

Tricky and/or new words in this book

Any words in bold may have unusual spellings
or are new and have not yet been introduced.

Tricky and/or new words in this book

> **worked diner wanted
> when busy there their
> came gave counter jukebox
> finer ate chowder the she**

Extra ways to have fun with this book

After the readers have finished the story, ask them
questions about what they have just read.

What did Dina do when the diner was busy?
What did Dina give T-Rex to eat at the diner?

Explain that the two letters *er* make one sound.
Think of other words that make the *er* sound,
such as *burger* and *finer*.

I'm a dinosaur,
but not a
veloci-rap-tor!

A Pronunciation Guide

This grid highlights the sounds used in the story and offers a guide on how to say them.

s	a	t	p	i
as in sat	as in ant	as in tin	as in pig	as in ink
n	c	e	h	r
as in net	as in cat	as in egg	as in hen	as in rat
m	d	g	o	u
as in mug	as in dog	as in get	as in ox	as in up
l	f	b	j	v
as in log	as in fan	as in bag	as in jug	as in van
w	z	y	k	qu
as in wet	as in zip	as in yet	as in kit	as in quick
x	ff	ll	ss	zz
as in box	as in off	as in ball	as in kiss	as in buzz
ck	pp	nn	rr	gg
as in duck	as in puppy	as in bunny	as in arrow	as in egg
dd	bb	tt	sh	ch
as in daddy	as in chubby	as in attic	as in shop	as in chip
th	th	ng	nk	le
as in them	as in the	as in sing	as in sunk	as in bottle
ai	ee	ie	oa	ue
as in rain	as in feet	as in pies	as in oak	as in cue
ar	er			
as in park	as in term			

Be careful not to add an /uh/ sound to /s/, /t/, /p/, /c/, /h/, /r/, /m/, /d/, /g/, /l/, /f/ and /b/. For example, say /ff/ not /fuh/ and /sss/ not /suh/.

Dina **worked** in **the diner**.
She wanted to be a rapper.

When it was **busy**,
she worked harder.

"Waiter, **there** is no butter." Dina zipped to get butter for **their** table.

"Waiter! I want **chowder**."
Dina was quick to bring it.

Dina wanted to be a rapper
but she did not fuss.

One day T-Rex **came** to the diner.
T-Rex was a rapper.

Dina was so happy. "Yes!"

Dina **gave** T-Rex a very
big burger.

She also gave him free pie,
extra fries, and lots of fizzy soda.

T-Rex just **ate** his burger.

He did not see Dina.

T-Rex put on his coat to go.

This was Dina's chance, her only shot at being a rapper. She had to think.

Dina turned on the **jukebox** and got on the **counter**.

She sang out, "I'm rapping in
my diner. Nothing else is **finer**!"

T-Rex loved Dina's rap.
Dina and T-Rex are both
rappers at the diner.

OVER **48** TITLES IN SIX LEVELS
Betty Franchi recommends...

Some titles from Level 1

I love reading phonics — **Bad Rat** — 978 1 84898 747 0

I love reading phonics — **The Best Gift** — 978 1 84898 750 0

I love reading phonics — **Clint and Grant Play I-Spy** — 978 1 84898 752 4

I love reading phonics — **Bret and Grandma's Trip!** — 978 1 84898 751 7

Some titles from Level 2

I love reading phonics — **Wish Fish** — 978 1 84898 755 5

I love reading phonics — **Chuck and Duck** — 978 1 84898 756 2

I love reading phonics — **Pink Bunny** — 978 1 84898 760 9

I love reading phonics — **Let's go to the Swings** — 978 1 84898 759 3

Other titles to enjoy from Level 3

I love reading phonics — **GOAT IN A BOAT** — 978 1 84898 766 1

I love reading phonics — **Queen Ella's Feet** — 978 1 84898 764 7

I love reading phonics — **Puff Flies** — 978 1 84898 765 4

An Hachette Company
First Published in the United States by TickTock, an imprint of Octopus Publishing Group.
www.octopusbooksusa.com

Copyright © Octopus Publishing Group Ltd 2013

Distributed in the US by
Hachette Book Group USA
237 Park Avenue, New York NY 10017, USA

Distributed in Canada by
Canadian Manda Group
165 Dufferin Street, Toronto, Ontario, Canada M6K 3H6

ISBN 978 1 84898 770 8

Printed and bound in China
10 9 8 7 6 5 4 3 2 1